Penguin WORKSHOP
An Imprint of Penguin Random House LLC, New York

Penguin supports copyright. Copyright fuels creativity, encourages diverse voices, promotes free speech, and creates a vibrant culture. Thank you for buying an authorized edition of this book and for complying with copyright laws by not reproducing, scanning, or distributing any part of it in any form without permission. You are supporting writers and allowing Penguin to continue to publish books for every reader.

Based on *The Day the Crayons Quit*, published in 2013 by Philomel Books, an imprint of Penguin Random House LLC. Text copyright © 2019 by Drew Daywalt. Illustrations copyright © 2013, 2019 by Oliver Jeffers. All rights reserved. Published in 2019 by Penguin Workshop, an imprint of Penguin Random House LLC, New York. PENGUIN and PENGUIN WORKSHOP are trademarks of Penguin Books Ltd, and the W colophon is a registered trademark of Penguin Random House LLC. Manufactured in China.

Visit us online at www.penguinrandomhouse.com.

ISBN 9781524792688   10 9 8

LOVE

FROM the CRAYONS

DREW DAYWALT
OLIVER JEFFERS

Penguin WORKSHOP

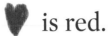 is red.

Because love comes in
all shapes and sizes.

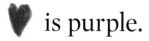 is purple.

Because love has
its own imagination.

is brown.

Because love is sweet
like chocolate.

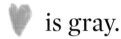 is gray.

Because love can be
small and soft,

or big and strong.

 is white.

Because sometimes
love is hard to see.

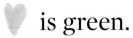 is green.

Because love is helpful.

is yellow and orange.

Because love is
sunny and warm.

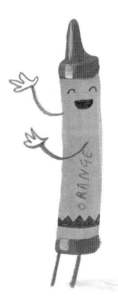

is blue.

Because sometimes
love is stormy.

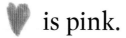 is pink.

Because love
can be silly.

is peach.

Because sometimes
love can hide.

is black.

Because love isn't always
bright and colorful.

 is every color!